This book belongs to

_____

Disney

Aladdin

The Story of Jasmine

Disney

Aladdin

The Story of Jasmine

Bath • New York • Cologne • Melbourne • Delhi
Hong Kong • Shenzhen • Singapore

This edition published by Parragon Books Ltd in 2018
and distributed by

Parragon Inc.
440 Park Avenue South, 13th Floor
New York, NY 10016
www.parragon.com

ISBN 978-1-5270-1877-8

Printed in China

See the good in others....

Good evening to you, worthy friend. This is no ordinary lamp. It once changed the course of a young man's life. A young man, who, like this lamp, was more than what he seemed—a Diamond in the Rough. Perhaps you would like to hear the tale?

It begins on a dark night . . . where an evil man waits with a dark purpose.

Deep in the Arabian Desert, an evil sorcerer named Jafar enlisted a thief to steal a golden scarab. Jafar eagerly touched the two halves of the magical object together. Glowing, it flew across the desert.

Jafar and the thief, Gazeem, quickly followed. Where the scarab stopped, an immense tiger head rose from the sand— the entrance to the Cave of Wonders.

Afraid to enter the cave himself, Jafar ordered Gazeem to
go. But as Gazeem moved toward the cave, the tiger boomed,
"Only one may enter here—the Diamond in the Rough!"
Gazeem hesitantly stepped inside. Suddenly, the tiger-head
entrance collapsed and Gazeem disappeared under the sand!
"I must find this one, this Diamond in the Rough," Jafar said.

Early the next morning, in the marketplace of
Agrabah, a boy named Aladdin took a loaf of bread.
    "Stop, thief!" shouted the Sultan's head palace guard.
With no parents to care for him, Aladdin had to steal
to eat.

Even though Aladdin had no money, he had a heart of gold. When a haughty prince tried to clear his way by hurting some children, Aladdin came to their rescue. "If I were as rich as you," Aladdin said, "I could afford some manners."

"You are a worthless street rat!" the prince said as he rode through the palace gates.

Aladdin and his pet monkey, Abu, trudged
to their rooftop home. Aladdin gazed at the
Sultan's palace. "Someday, Abu, things are
gonna change. We'll be rich, live in a palace,
and never have any problems at all."

At the palace, Princess Jasmine had a problem. Her father, the Sultan, said the law required that she marry a prince by her next birthday—in only three days! But Jasmine didn't like any of the princes her father presented to her. She wanted to marry for love. The Sultan didn't understand.

Jasmine explained to her father that she had never done anything on her own. She'd never had any real friends, except for her tiger, Rajah. She hadn't been outside the palace walls. Maybe she didn't even want to be a princess anymore! Feeling trapped, Jasmine set her doves free and watched them fly.

Alone in his throne room, the Sultan wondered what he should do about his daughter. Suddenly, a shadow loomed over him. The Sultan smiled cheerfully at his visitor. "Ah, Jafar, my most trusted advisor. I am in desperate need of your wisdom."

Jafar told the Sultan he could help, but he would need the Sultan's Mystic Blue Diamond ring to do so. Before the Sultan could ask why, Jafar hypnotized him long enough to get the ring.

Now Jafar could use the ring to find the mysterious Diamond in the Rough.

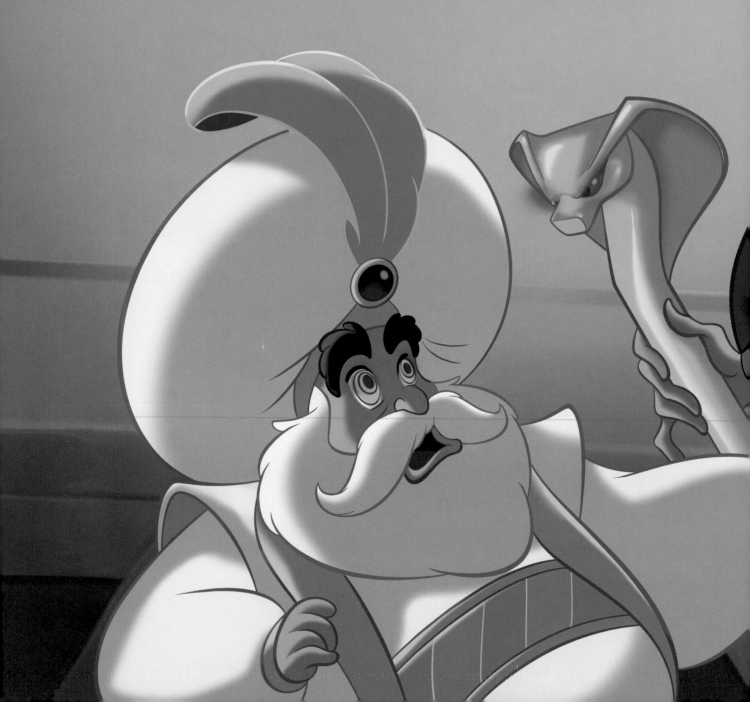

While Jafar plotted and planned, Jasmine
decided she would rather leave her life as a
princess than be forced to marry.

"I'm sorry, Rajah," she said to her tiger. "But I can't stay here and have my life lived for me. I'll miss you."

She climbed over the palace wall and was gone.

The next morning, Jasmine wandered into the marketplace, delighted by the sights and sounds. Her striking beauty caught Aladdin's attention.

He watched Jasmine take an apple and give it to a child without paying. Having never been out in the world, Jasmine didn't realize she was stealing.

"Thief!" shouted the vendor.

While Jasmine tried to explain herself, Aladdin leapt to her aid. He convinced the vendor that Jasmine wasn't a thief. She was just lost and confused.

They managed to walk away unharmed.

Meanwhile, in his secret chamber, Jafar used the Sultan's diamond ring to activate the Sands of Time.

"Reveal to me the one who can enter the cave," he commanded the magical hourglass. "There he is . . . my Diamond in the Rough."

The sands showed Aladdin! Jafar ordered guards to bring him to the palace.

Back at Aladdin's home, Jasmine was impressed with where Aladdin lived.

"It's not much," Aladdin said, "but it's got a great view."

When Jasmine saw the palace in the distance, the smile fell from her face.

"Where are you from?" Aladdin asked.

"What does it matter?" she said. "I ran away, and I am not going back."

Suddenly, the palace guards thundered up the stairs, interrupting their conversation. "Here you are!" shouted a guard.

"They're after me!" Jasmine and Aladdin cried in unison.

The pair tried to get away, but the guards managed to catch Aladdin. Jasmine threw off her scarf, revealing her royal identity. "Unhand him," she said, "by order of the princess!"

"I would, Princess," said the captain, who was shocked to see her, "except my orders come from Jafar."

The guards locked Aladdin and Abu in a deserted dungeon. Aladdin couldn't help feeling frustrated about Jasmine. She was a princess! No matter how much he liked her, he'd never see her again. He was a street rat, and she deserved a prince.

Just then, an old man appeared. He offered to make Aladdin rich—rich enough to impress a princess—if Aladdin would do one small errund for him. When the old man opened a secret passage that led out of the dungeon, Aladdin agreed to help.

The old man took Aladdin and Abu to the Cave of Wonders.
He wanted Aladdin to retrieve a magical item for him.
"Who disturbs my slumber?" the tiger-head entrance roared.
"It is I, Aladdin," he said.
"Proceed," the tiger thundered. "Touch nothing but the lamp!"

Aladdin and Abu entered a huge treasure chamber.
A magic carpet playfully tugged at Abu's tail, then hid
behind a pile of gold.

"Maybe you can help us," Aladdin said to the carpet as
he looked around. "See, we're trying to find this lamp."

The carpet led Aladdin and Abu to a lake deep in the cave. At its center was a huge altar of rocks with a lamp on top. Aladdin crossed the lake and crept up a set of stairs. He carefully approached the lamp— but it didn't look all that impressive.

Just then, Abu saw a statue holding a glowing gem.
He had to have it!
"Abu! No!" Aladdin shouted from the top of the stairs.
Even the carpet tried to stop Abu. But it was too late.

"You have touched the forbidden treasure!" the
tiger thundered.

The ground rumbled and shook. Aladdin was
flung into the air. The cave floor turned to molten
lava. The carpet caught Aladdin and Abu and
raced toward the cave entrance.

But before they could escape, Aladdin fell.
Frantically, he grabbed for a handhold, begging
the old man for help.

"First give me the lamp!" the man said.
Aladdin handed it over . . .

. . . only to be betrayed. The old man had no intention of helping Aladdin or Abu. They both fell to the bottom of the cavern.

The old man reached inside his cloak for the precious lamp only to realize it was gone! He howled in rage! Ripping off his beard, the old man revealed he was actually Jafar in disguise.

Thanks to the Magic Carpet, Aladdin and Abu landed
safely in the cave, which had turned back into stone. They
were trapped, but at least Abu had stolen back the lamp.

Aladdin rubbed the lamp to get a better look. Suddenly, sparks flew, smoke swirled, and *poof*—a genie appeared!

"So what'll it be, Master?" the Genie asked. He explained that Aladdin could have three wishes. Aladdin didn't know what to wish for.

The Genie explained he was the best friend Aladdin could ask for. He could give him riches, the most magnificent food, and strength beyond words! But there were limitations to the wishes.

"Limitations?" Aladdin smiled at Abu. "He probably can't even get us out of this cave."

"Excuse me?" said the Genie.

Seconds later, they were flying
free on the Magic Carpet—without
having used any of Aladdin's wishes.

Meanwhile, Jasmine was angry with Jafar. She believed that he had gotten rid of Aladdin forever. The Sultan tried to make peace between the two. Jafar apologized, but Jasmine would have none of it.

"At least some good will come of my being forced to marry," Jasmine said. "When I am queen, I will have the power to get rid of you!"

Safely out of the cave, Aladdin thought about his first wish. He wanted to be with Jasmine. "Genie, I wish for you to make me a prince!"

The Genie looked at Aladdin's size and build. He measured here . . .

. . . and there. And then, with a wave of his big blue hands . . .

. . . Presto! The Genie had dressed Aladdin in clothes fit
for a prince. "Hang on to your turban, kid!" the Genie
announced. "We're gonna make you a star!"

In the blink of an eye, Aladdin found himself riding into Agrabah in a spectacular parade of acrobats, dancers, and sword twirlers, along with a menagerie of animals—including Abu, whom the Genie had changed into an elephant.

Arriving at the palace, Aladdin—as Prince Ali Ababwa—asked for Jasmine's hand in marriage. The Sultan was delighted. Jasmine, who did not recognize Aladdin, was not impressed. She wasn't a prize to be won.

That night, Aladdin knew he needed to fix
things with Jasmine. "I gotta be smooth, cool,
confident," he told himself. Then he got on his
carpet and floated up to her balcony.

"Princess Jasmine?" Aladdin called.

"Who's there?"

"It's me, uh . . . Prince Ali Ababwa."

"Just leave me alone!" Jasmine responded.
Rajah growled at him.

"Wait," Jasmine said. "Do I know you?"
Aladdin didn't confess the truth. Jasmine
turned away. She had little interest in a
stuck-up prince. Then he told her what he
thought about her future: "You should be free
to make your own choice." With that, and a
peek at the Magic Carpet, she couldn't resist
his offer of a ride.

Flying over deserts, mountains, and seas, past cities and countrysides, they discovered a whole new world together. Jasmine discovered even more: as she had suspected, Prince Ali was actually the boy from the market!

By the time Aladdin returned Jasmine to the palace, she had decided he was the one for her.

"Good night, my handsome prince," she whispered, leaving Aladdin feeling as if he were floating on air. For the first time in his life, things were starting to go right.

But Jafar had an evil plan
for Aladdin!

"I'm afraid you've worn
out your welcome, Prince
Abooboo," Jafar said. He
ordered the palace guards
to bind Aladdin and throw
him into the sea!

Aladdin sank to the bottom of the sea, and the lamp landed nearby. He struggled to reach it, but he was running out of air. Luckily, he bumped into the lamp at last. By the time the Genie appeared, Aladdin had lost consciousness.

The Genie used one of Aladdin's
wishes to rescue him. Then he took
Aladdin safely to shore. He was alive!

At the palace, Jafar had hypnotized the Sultan again. Turning to Jasmine, the Sultan commanded, "You will wed Jafar."

Just then, Aladdin arrived and revealed Jafar as an evil sorcerer. Jafar caught sight of Aladdin's lamp and realized who Prince Ali really was, just before the villain vanished into thin air.

Not long after, Jafar's parrot, Iago, lured
Aladdin outside by mimicking Jasmine's
voice. When Aladdin went looking for her,
Iago stole the lamp and gave it to Jafar.

After Jafar rubbed the lamp, he told the Genie his first command:
"I wish to rule on high as Sultan!"

The Genie had to obey. He transformed Jafar into the Sultan. Then the Genie lifted the palace into the air.

"Genie! No!" Aladdin shouted.

"Sorry, kid. I've got a new master now," replied the Genie.

Jafar made his second wish: to be the most powerful sorcerer in the world. He told Jasmine that Aladdin wasn't a real prince. Then Jafar exiled the boy far, far away. Aladdin and Abu huddled in the cold. "Somehow, I gotta go back and set things right," Aladdin said.

Back at the palace, Jafar had strung
up the Sultan like a puppet and made
Jasmine his slave.

Luckily, the Magic Carpet went to Aladdin's rescue once more and flew him back to the palace. When Jasmine caught sight of Aladdin sneaking in, she pretended to flirt with Jafar. If only she could distract him long enough for Aladdin to save her and her father!

But Aladdin's rescue attempt failed.
The wicked sorcerer used his magic to
imprison Jasmine in a giant hourglass and
turn Abu into a toy.

Then he trapped Aladdin behind a wall of swords!
But the street rat was ready to improvise.

Aladdin grabbed one of the swords.
"Are you afraid to fight me yourself, you
cowardly snake?" he shouted.

"Perhaps you'd like to see how
snakelike I can be," Jafar replied as he
morphed into an enormous cobra.

Then Aladdin had an idea.
"The Genie has more power than you'll
ever have!" he taunted Jafar.
    Infuriated, Jafar used his final wish.
"I wish to be an all-powerful genie!"

Jafar was instantly transformed
into a genie. But he had forgotten
that a genie is doomed to live in a
lamp and obey a master's wishes.
   Aladdin picked up Jafar's lamp—
and Jafar was imprisoned inside it for
all time. The Genie then threw the
lamp deep into the desert.

As a reward for Aladdin's bravery, the Sultan changed the law so Jasmine could marry whomever she chose.

Aladdin used his third wish to free the Genie. Aladdin and the Genie hugged good-bye, but they knew they would be friends forever.